The Further
TALE OF
PETER
RABBIT

"*Aye,*" said a deep voice, "*no matter where we've
been or where we're going, 'tis the hills draw us back.*"

THE *Further* TALE OF
PETER RABBIT

BY

Emma Thompson

ILLUSTRATED BY

Eleanor Taylor

FREDERICK WARNE

FOR PETER
CHILDHOOD FRIEND
LEGEND
RABBIT

FREDERICK WARNE

Published by the Penguin Group
Penguin Books Ltd, 80 Strand, London WC2R ORL, England
Penguin Young Readers Group, 345 Hudson Street, New York, New York 10014, USA
Penguin Group (Canada), 90 Eglinton Avenue East,
Suite 700, Toronto, Ontario, Canada M4P 2Y3
Penguin Ireland, 25 St Stephen's Green, Dublin 2, Ireland
Penguin Group (Australia), 250 Camberwell Road, Camberwell, Victoria 3124, Australia
Penguin Books India (P) Ltd, 11 Community Centre,
Panchsheel Park, New Delhi 110 017, India
Penguin Group (NZ), 67 Apollo Drive, Rosedale, North Shore 0632, New Zealand
Penguin Books (South Africa) (Pty) Ltd, PO Box 9, Parklands 2121, South Africa

Penguin Books Ltd, Registered Offices: 80 Strand, London WC2R ORL, England

www.peterrabbit.com

First published by Frederick Warne 2012

001-1 2 3 4 5 6 7 8 9 10

Printed and bound in China

Dear Reader,

On a hot (ish) day in Scotland, during what many persisted in calling the 'summer' of 2010, I received a package from an old childhood acquaintance. Surprisingly fresh in my memory, I knew him to be wise yet rash, funny yet dignified and always up to something.

His two most remarkable qualities were that he was 110 years old and a rabbit. The parcel contained some half-eaten radish-tops and a letter inviting me to write a new tale.

He observed in his missive that I was 'a tad naughty', even 'mischievous' – neither of which rang any bells with me or my family (who know me to be a sober, quiet individual who shies away from attention).

Nonetheless it was an invitation I could no more refuse than I could refuse to breathe.

The following pages contain the fruit of that damp season's labour and I wish you the same joy in reading them as I took in writing them.

-E. T.

I HAVE NOT SEEN many rabbits
moping, but when they do, their
ears droop.

PETER RABBIT was in low spirits. It had been a rainy summer, his blue coat had been torn by briars and his shoes were hurting.

"What I need," he said, *"is a change of scene."*

Benjamin Bunny advised against it. *"Too many carts on the road,"* he said. *"Too many owls, and too many foxes."*

DISCOURAGED, Peter squeezed under the gate into Mr. McGregor's garden, intending to steal a lettuce.

What should he find by the greenhouse but an interesting basket smelling of onions?

He opened it and climbed in.

INSIDE, wrapped in brown paper, were some excellent sandwiches of cheese and pickle.

He ate them all.

It was cosy in the basket so he fell asleep.

WHEN he woke up the basket was *joggling*. Fearfully, Peter lifted the lid and peeked out.

The basket was in a cart and the cart was on the open road!

Badly frightened, and with no idea of what to do, Peter shot under the neatly folded blanket on the bottom.

THE joggling went on for a
very
    very
       very
           Long Time.

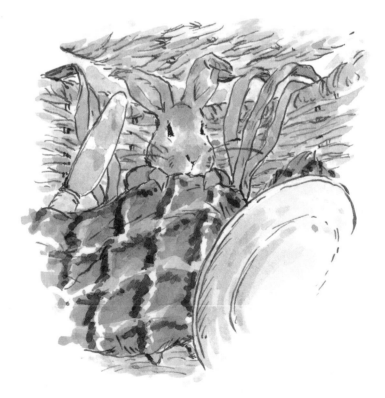

WHEN it stopped, someone lifted the lid of the basket.

"*Who's eaten our picnic?*" screeched Mrs. McGregor, twitching away the blanket.

"*THIEF!!*" she screamed.

Peter bolted just in time.

HE ran until he could run no more. Panting at the foot of a tall pine-tree, he looked about. A stream ran clear over mossy grey stones, harebells bobbing at the rim.

The call of a buzzard made him look up in fright to see high purple hills. Peter, who had a sore paw from running, limped out and stared. He had left his shoes in the basket.

"A<small>YE</small>," said a deep voice, *"no matter where we've been or where we're going, 'tis the hills draw us back."*

Peter turned to see a HUGE black rabbit in a kilt, a dagger thrust into the top of his laced-up boot.

"Ye'll *be Peter Rabbit*," said the giant. Peter nodded.

"*Finlay McBurney at your service. News of your disappearance came up with the mail-coach. Your mother's fit to be tied. Follow me.*"

Peter followed. He thought it better not to mention the sandwich-basket.

THE Scottish burrow was hung with bunches of bog-cotton.

The peat on the fire smelt sharp. Mrs. McBurney, her ears tied in a neat knot, met Peter with a bowl of steaming porridge.

HE was put to bed with much
kindness, on a sack filled with
sheepswool and heather.

WHEN he woke, Mrs. McBurney had made potato scones for his breakfast.

"*Hurry now dearie,*" she said.

"*Today's the Big Day! Finlay's defending his title!*"

"*Oh, good,*" said Peter, not wishing to appear ignorant – even though he had no idea what '*defending his title*' meant.

In a clearing not far from the burrow, rabbits from all the different clans were gathering.

At last, Finlay appeared holding up a great golden cup. "*I challenge all comers!*" he bellowed.

Peter thought it was very exciting.

THE Games began.

Most of them involved throwing
something heavy as far as possible.
Finlay won nearly all of them.

Quite soon, Peter thought it very
boring.

To the side, the bracken was flattened into a path, which Peter followed, cautiously.

He came upon a sign, which read "KEEP OUT."

I imagine it will not surprise you to hear that Peter
did not
KEEP OUT.

He WENT IN.

THERE, protected by willow-fencing,
lay an *unusually* large RADISH.

IT must have measured three rabbits round! It also smelt delicious and Peter was very hungry.

He thought no-one would notice if he took a little nibble off the end.

Accordingly, he scratched his way under the willow-fence and took a bite.
    And then,
        another.
            And another.

BY the time Peter had stopped eating, he was INSIDE the radish.

Feeling cosy, he fell asleep.

When he woke up, the radish
was
joggling.

"*Not again*," thought Peter.

ALL of a sudden, the radish was tipped up and Peter tumbled out.

HE found himself back in the clearing. All the rabbits were shouting "*Throw the radish! Throw the radish!*"

"*Young cousin Peter!*" boomed Finlay. "*Be a good wee bunny and toss me yon radish!*"

This was unfair.

Finlay knew the radish was far too heavy for a little rabbit to throw all by himself. But he did not know that most of the radish was *inside* Peter.

PETER picked the radish up by its top-knot. Everyone laughed at him.

Peter whirled the radish around his head and let go.

It flew clean over Finlay and landed with a thud on the other side of the clearing.

Everyone stopped laughing.

THEN a rabbit in a tam o'shanter yelled, "*Peter Rabbit wins the Cup!*"

Peter was raised aloft on dozens of rough paws and bounced about until he felt sick.

I am sorry to say that he had eaten far too much radish.

WHEN they put him down, Finlay came up with the Cup. "*Aye, ye've won fair and square, laddie!*" he said. "*The Cup is yours!*"

Peter felt awful.

"*I didn't win it fair and square!*" he exclaimed.

He told Finlay the truth about the hollow radish. When he'd finished, there was a *long* silence.

FINALLY, Finlay threw back his ears and roared with laughter.

Finlay kept his Golden Cup and Peter's clever trick became the greatest story in the history of the Games.

THEY all feasted on young turnips and the remains of the radish.

Everyone was *very* cheerful, but Peter was homesick.

THE very next day, Finlay hid him behind a sack of letters on the mail-coach south. Mrs. McBurney had mended his blue jacket and given him a fat little haggis for his mother.

"*Haste ye back, wee Cousin Peter*," said Finlay. Then he coughed and turned away. Something seemed to have got into his eye.

Peter thought it was a midge.

THERE was great rejoicing in the sand-bank when Peter arrived home. His mother had worn herself to a *frazzle* in his absence.

She did not mention the shoes.

PETER was made to tell the story of the giant radish again and again. Benjamin Bunny always paid it particular attention.

One morning, as the first leaves were turning, he crept up beside Peter.

"Um...next time you need a change of scene," he said. *"Can I come?"*

THE END